Mitsumasa Anno

IN SHADOWLAND

ORCHARD BOOKS
A Division of Franklin Watts, Inc.
New York

Copyright and Library of Congress Cataloging-in-Publication information at end of book

Everything has a shadow.
A shadow has a shape and is black,
but it has no substance, weight or
thickness. Suppose there was a
land of shadows. . . . All the shadows
in the world could come there and yet
there would be room for everyone.
There would be no population
problems or racial differences.
What a happy place that would be!
But even in Shadowland there might
be both good and evil things, who
knows? Here in this book are some
of my ideas about shadows. I would
like to visit Shadowland myself.
Will you come with me?

Mitsumasa Anno

1 It was winter again in the town. The sky was dark and
gray. The sun had not been seen for weeks. A cold wind
had blown all the leaves off the trees. Softly, snow
began to fall in the quiet streets.

It was winter in Shadowland, too. In the summertime, when the sun shone, the shadows had to take their places out in the world. But in the dark winters they ran happily back to Shadowland.

1

2 On this dark and snowy night, it was so cold that even the air seemed frozen. A little girl stood all alone in the center of the town. She was a match-seller, but it was late and there were no customers out on the cold streets.

In Shadowland, too, the streets were empty. Only the watchman was out of doors. He guarded the gates of Shadowland. No one could enter there except shadows, and the shadows could not leave in the dark winter season. Only the watchman could come and go as he pleased.

2

3

In the town, the little match girl still had not sold a single
box of matches. Her feet were bare, for a carriage had
knocked her down, and a naughty boy had run off with her
shoes. Now she shivered in the icy wind.

A few weeks earlier, the watchman had welcomed the shadows back
to their hidden land. They sang and danced as they came back
with their animals and their tools and other possessions. They
looked forward to spending a jolly winter together.

3

4 It was so cold that the little match girl could not resist taking out one match and lighting it. The flame was tiny but warm. Then, to her surprise, she heard a voice from somewhere saying, "Cheer up! Don't cry!" But she couldn't see anyone in the dark, snowy street. "Perhaps I only imagined it," she thought.

In Shadowland, the watchman was peering through a long telescope. It was his job to ring the alarm bell and warn the shadows if ever he saw even a faint sign of the sun. For then they would have to go back out into the world. Now he didn't see the sun, but he saw a tiny flame far off in the city—and he saw the poor little match girl there.

4

The girl struck another match. Then, suddenly, she saw a handsome young man in a red coat coming down the street. He bought a whole box of her matches, and began to light them, one by one. And as he did so, shadows of the girl and the young man sprang out against the snow. The shadows were black and clear like the shadows on a warm summer day.

5

Back in Shadowland, the shadows were having a party. You might think that
shadows would sit still and be quiet when they were back in their secret
place. But oh, no! They were never quiet. How could they be when their
musicians played their instruments and the dancers tried new steps?
It was like a festival every day.

5

6 The young man struck another match—and another, and another! They flashed like fireworks, making shadows of the lamp post, of the well, and even of a little dog that passed by. Now people began peering out of windows, curious to see the bright flames and pretty shadows in the middle of winter.

Back in Shadowland, more shadows continued to arrive. It looked like a
carnival. There were shadows of reindeer, of storks and swallows.
There were shadows of elephants and alligators and monkeys. There was
even the shadow of a pyramid!

6

7 In the town, everyone was buying matches from the little girl and lighting them. How surprising it was to see such lovely shadows, even on a dark winter's night! It was almost like spring! Even the little girl felt quite warm, although the snow was still falling and the cold wind was still blowing.

But back in Shadowland, the alarm bell began to ring loudly. Roosters crowed, ducks quacked, foxes yelped. From parrots to children, from children to mothers, from mothers to fathers the news spread until it reached the king of the shadows. "The watchman is gone!" "We can't find the watchman!"

7

8   As more and more matches were sold, the town grew brighter and
    brighter. There was great excitement. Everyone now had shadows,
    and the shadows did not try to run away to Shadowland.

In Shadowland, too, there was great excitement. There was no more music and dancing. Everyone was looking for the watchman. Bird shadows flew around the land, searching for him.

8

9 Suddenly, in the town, the people began to point to the match girl
and the watchman and to shout, "Look! They must be witches!" For behind
the match girl and the watchman, their two shadows had joined together
and formed a single shadow that looked like a witch. "Catch them!"
cried the townspeople.

Meantime, in Shadowland, everyone was searching for the watchman. "He went this way!" some shadows shouted. "No, *that* way!" said others. "How will we know when it is time for us to take our places in the world?" shrieked a shadow-monkey, who had turned bright red from fright. "The king will be angry if we don't go when we're needed."

9

10 Now everyone in the town began chasing the match girl and the watchman.
"We're not witches! It's just a mistake! You have to believe us!"
cried the watchman, but no one listened to him.

The king of Shadowland told his people, "Please don't worry. I won't punish anyone. It is not your fault if you don't know when to go out into the world." But the shadow people were not comforted. "We want our watchman back," they said.

10

11 The watchman and the match girl ran through towns, through villages, over fields, across rivers, over hills and mountains. They ran to Shadowland.

In Shadowland, the people had climbed up on the watch tower and on the high mountain, and they were shouting, "Please come back, watchman! We need you!"

11

12   The big black raven saw them first. "The watchman's back," he called out.
Roosters crowed, ducks quacked, foxes yelped. From parrots to children, from

children to mothers, from mothers to fathers, from fathers to the king, the good
news spread. It was the happiest day there had ever been in Shadowland.

12

13 The king was the happiest of all. He completely forgot that he had been angry with the watchman for leaving his post. "Don't just stand around

talking," he said to his courtiers. "Can't you see that the watchman has brought back his bride-to-be? We must get ready for the wedding!"

And so the watchman and the little match girl were married and they lived happily ever after. At least, that is the way they tell the story in Shadowland.

Do you think it is true?

Library of Congress Cataloging-in-Publication Data
Anno, Mitsumasa, 1926–   In shadowland.   Translation of: Kagebōshi.
Summary: Chaos descends on Shadowland when the watchman leaves his post to join a little
match girl on a snowy street in the real world.   [1. Shadows—Fiction] I. Title.
PZ7.A5875In 1988   [E]   87-20362   ISBN 0-531-05741-0   ISBN 0-531-08341-1 (lib. bdg.)

The publishers wish to thank Ann Herring and Yumiko Sakuma for their
assistance with the translation of this story from the Japanese.
English translation copyright © 1988 by Orchard Books, New York.
Original Japanese text and illustrations copyright © 1976 by Kuso-Kubo.
First published as KAGEBŌSHI in 1976 by Fuzambo Publishing Co., Tokyo. American translation rights arranged
through Japan Foreign Rights Centre. All rights reserved. No part of this book may be reproduced or transmitted
in any form or by any means, electronic or mechanical, including photocopying, recording or by any information
storage or retrieval system, without permission in writing from the publisher.
Orchard Books
387 Park Avenue South
New York, New York 10016
Orchard Books Canada
20 Torbay Road
Markham, Ontario 23P 1G6
Orchard Books is a division of Franklin Watts, Inc.
Manufactured in the United States of America.